The Birth

Daisy Mulhern lay back in her pram sucking her soother as she began to think back on the first six months of her life. Even now her eyes filled with tears as she remembered the first words that she had ever heard spoken. It was the moment of her birth six months ago at the Charlemont Hospital.

'Strange looking little yoke', were the words used to describe her, as a nurse yanked her out into a bright light. The remark was made by a bald man with a large tummy whom she now knew to be her dad, Bill Mulhern. 'That's rich coming from him,' thought Daisy, as she looked over at him standing beside the bed. 'He is not exactly a pin-up himself.' He was busy mopping the brow of a large lady with a very red face, who was puffing and panting. Dottie didn't realise until later that this was her mother, Dottie Mulhern.

'Its a girl!' said the nurse excitedly, 'and there is another baby on the way!' She dropped Daisy like a hot potato on the bed and started yanking Daisy's twin brother, poor little Dessie, out into the horribly bright light. He looked very much the worse for the wear.

'I don't think he is breathing,' said another nurse, as she whacked poor Dessie across his rump and he started to bawl. Daisy looked at the nurse with disgust.

'How would she like someone to ... no! Better not to think about it.' Poor Dessie got such a shock that he continued to bawl but worse was to come. They were

THE MULHERN TWINS

Mary Gallagher

MARY GALLAGHER is a former primary school
teacher. She is married with four children and
has written plays for the primary schools
drama festival and teenage plays for her local
youth club, as well as a novel for children –
The Snot Gang in 'Gotcha'.

The Collins Press

Published in 2006 by
The Collins Press
West Link Park
Doughcloyne
Wilton
Cork

© Mary Gallagher 2006
© Illustrations Deirdre O'Neill 2006

Mary Gallagher has asserted her moral right to be identified
as author of this work.

A CIP record for this book is available from the British library

ISBN-10: 1-905172-17-6
ISBN-13: 978-1905172-7

Typesetting: The Collins Press

Font: Comic Sans MS, 14 point

Cover design and illustrations: Deirdre O'Neill

Printed in Ireland by ColourBooks Ltd

Dedication
S.H.J.I.H.M.

both wrapped in sheets, one on each side of the large lady, whose name was Dottie.

'Congratulations Mrs Mulhern,' the nurse said cheerfully. 'You have a baby son and daughter – a fine pair of twins.' Dottie was crying slightly hysterically.

'Oh! It runs in families you know. I have a twin sister, Lottie. We are identical.' Daisy peeped out from under the sheet.

'Imagine, there are two of her,' she thought. 'What a horrible thought.'

At the bottom of the bed stood the same bald man who had said 'funny looking yoke' earlier. The twins later found out that his name was Bill Mulhern. Apparently this specimen was their dad. He stood there mopping his brow as if he too had just run a marathon.

'Am I glad that is all over,' he sighed. 'I am knackered.'

'Why?' wondered the twins. He had done nothing. In fact he looked as if he never did anything apart from feel sorry for himself. Just as well the twins weren't

the sensitive type! The nurse even had to prompt him to admire them.

'Pretty little things, aren't they?' she remarked.

'THINGS!' The twins chose to ignore that remark. 'How dare she!'

With great reluctance, Mr Mulhern answered that as babies go he supposed they were alright. He didn't sound as if he was convinced. Mind you, pretty wasn't a term the twins would use themselves!

4

They were raw and red with two scrunched up faces. Not exactly material for a bonny baby show! But then, one had to consider where they came from!

For nine months the twins had lain all cosy and warm inside their mother. They felt safe in there until today, when Daisy could feel herself being pulled away from Dessie and being pushed down a long tube. She didn't want to go but was forced along. Eventually she could see bright lights in the distance and a lot of scream-ing. Daisy was terrified and wanted to go back but she was forced to continue. The nurse had pulled her into the light and the horror that went with it. Did she get any sympathy? No! All the sympathy seemed to go to her new mum, Dottie Mulhern.

With Dad's lack of interest it was to Dottie, their mum that the twins turned to for comfort. After all, that is what mums are supposed to do, aren't they? After a quick look at her newborns she mumbled sleepily, 'a bit yellow, aren't they? Still I am glad that is over! Could you take them away now nurse, I could do with a good sleep!'

'Oh, thanks a bunch!' thought the twins, 'that really makes us feel wanted.'

They were carried off to the nursery where they were washed and weighed. They felt a bit like two Christmas turkeys being prepared for the oven. The twins were then put into two glass cribs once they were washed and powdered.

Daisy opened her eyes to take a look at her newly-bathed brother. 'Ugly little git', was her first reaction, but then she remembered what the nurse had said.

'They are so alike, no one could tell the difference'. Suddenly tears welled up in Daisy's eyes.

'How could she look like that sad little git in the cot next to her'?

With those thoughts in mind Daisy slept her first night on this world at the Charlemont Maternity Hospital, in the next crib to her brand new twin brother, Dessie.

First Impressions

The twins awoke the following morning to hear a nurse saying another, 'Poor little mites. Imagine being born on 29 February. They will only have a birthday every four years and then, to have to go home to that dreadful Mulhern family. I wouldn't give my dog to that couple.'

This was the first inkling the twins had that life from now on was not going to be all sunshine.

'Did you hear that?' hissed Dessie from his crib? 'Pity we can't run away.'

Daisy feared the worst. She had a strange feeling from the time that she first saw Bill and Dottie Mulhern that something was not right. But worse was to follow!

'Do you know if Mrs Mulhern is breast-feeding?' asked the prettier of the two nurses. Daisy and Dessie looked at each other in alarm. It seemed an age before the other nurse replied.

'No!' It seemed that Dottie Mulhern was not the maternal type. She wanted the babies bottle fed so that husband Bill could play his part in feeding them. The twins were so overcome with relief that they started to cry.

'There, there! Don't cry,' said one of the nurses kindly, as she and the other nurse lifted a twin each. A lovely smell of perfume came from the nurses' uniforms.

'Why can't our mum smell and act like they do?' thought Daisy, wistfully.

Both babies were fed and changed. Dessie could feel his face going red. After all, he was a boy and it should be understood that most boys like privacy in the company of females. He was glad when he was fully dressed and back in his crib, all comfy and warm.

Most mothers are anxious to see their newborn baby first thing in the morning but not so Dottie Mulhern. Dessie could hear one nurse say to the other, 'Imagine! She told me to keep them in the nursery as long as possible as she needs her beauty sleep!'

'Boy! Does she need it!' thought Dessie but was too polite to make any baby noises to relay his thoughts to Daisy.

'Do you think she might be suffering from post-natal depression so soon after birth?' enquired the other nurse.

'Hardly likely! If you ask me she has no interest whatsoever in those two poor little mites. My heart does out to them.' Dessie and Daisy heard every word and tears welled up in their eyes.

It was now time for the twins to take stock of the other babies in the nursery.

Dessie had already whispered a shy 'hello' in baby language to a little ginger haired baby boy to his left side and he appeared to be quite friendly. Further over was a baby girl with a large mop of blonde hair and to Daisy's right was a baby girl who hadn't one hair on her head! Daisy giggled as she and Dessie secretly called them 'Ginger', 'Hairy' and 'Baldy'. 'Ginger' already had been taken out at first light to his mother, who was in what the nurses called, a 'Private Ward'. 'Hairy' had just been born that morning and was lying in shock at the new strange world that was opening up around her. 'Baldy' turned to be quite a chatterbox. Within half an hour the twins had discovered that she had eight brothers and sisters and that she was going to live on a farm, whatever that was. However, it was from the lively chatter of the nurses that the twins got most of their information.

'His mum thinks he is the bees knees', was a comment the nurses made about

Ginger's mum. Apparently Ginger's old pair were also filthy rich.

'Lucky little sod!' thought Daisy, 'I bet he will have a few birthdays every year, whatever they are.' Her lips quivered as she thought of how she and Dessie were so unlucky. Baldy's family would arrive later in the afternoon to see their mother. Apparently they were all excited and could hardly wait.

'Would have thought at this stage that one more child won't make much difference,' nattered on the nurse but she was assured by the other nurse that Baldy's family just loved babies.

'I wonder how they will all get here,' thought Dessie. 'I expect they'll have to hire a bus.'

Hairy was a greedy gut and had already been fed twice. Dessie liked her right-away. Daisy looked with envy over at her blonde hair and wondered if she would ever have hair.

'Hairy' had been two weeks overdue so

her older brother, aged four had given up on his family ever getting a new baby. Apparently his dad was having quite a job convincing him that at long last the promised baby had arrived.

Just then the nurse arrived in smiling.

'Well, babies! It's time we brought you all out to the wards to meet your mums!'

A friendly young nurse smiled at the twins and wheeled them both out to the ward. Mrs Mulhern was propped up on two pillows, her hair full of rollers and she was stuffing her face with chocolates.

'Oh no! Can't you keep them another while?' she wailed. 'I just knew this was too good to last'.

The nurse looked at her with disgust and left the cribs beside her with a bottle of warm milk and a nappy in each crib. As Dottie fed the twins, she continued to guzzle one chocolate after another. Poor Daisy's mouth watered.

'Just my luck,' thought Dottie Mulhern. 'I get a baby that dribbles.' She wiped

12

Daisy's mouth roughly with a hanky. As she changed their nappies she complained aloud.

'Don't think for one minute that the pair of you are going to stop me going to Bingo.' The twins wondered what she meant. How could they stop her going anywhere? And what was Bingo? Dessie's eyes watered as she rubbed cream roughly on his bottom.

'Not another whinger like the Mulherns,' she muttered. 'Oh, you are your dad's son alright.' The nurse had been right. Daisy and Dessie wished they could run away but their short legs were powerless. They were stuck with Dotty Mulhern for better or worse. As she fixed them in their crib her mood improved.

'Let's hope your sisters Gertie and Nellie have your room ready for you.'

'Seems we are not the only ones in the family then,' hissed Dessie to Daisy in baby language. Then, he continued, in a more hopeful voice, 'Maybe they will like us.'

'I hope so,' replied Daisy, feeling not

13

too sure.

'Oh, look! It will soon be visiting time!' said Dottie Mulhern, 'I must make myself pretty'.

'Dream on!' thought Dessie as he watched, fascinated, from his glass crib.

Dottie Mulhern sat on the bed and spread two, large hairy legs on the bed-spread. Then she took out a small bottle in which there was a shocking pink coloured liquid and she painted this on her rather odd toenails. While her toes were drying she plastered a thick brown liquid on to her face and pulled hairs from her eyebrows with a little silver thing. Dessie could feel his own eyebrows getting sore. Then Dottie pulled more hairs from her chin and sprayed a sickening cloud of perfume all around her person. Dessie and Daisy started to cough and splutter. They were terrified and thought they were going to choke.

'Aw, shut up, the pair of you,' she scolded. 'Just like the Mulherns – they always were a wheezy lot!' The hurtful remarks brought tears to Dessie and Daisy's eyes. Luckily, a kind nurse came in.

'Mrs Mulhern, whatever are you doing? That spray is not good for babies,' she scolded.

'They will just have to get used to it, won't they?' Dottie replied sharply, as she shrugged her shoulders in a careless attitude. She then continued to take the rollers out of her hair. She went to the bathroom next and when she returned she looked like something that had escaped from the circus – at least that's what Daisy heard one nurse say to the other when she saw Dottie come up the ward.

Dotty Mulhern staggered up in a shocking pink nylon negligee which matched the lipstick and nail polish. Her white, hairy legs were stuffed into a pair of tiny purple slippers that were definitely not made to house the ten heavily painted toes that peeped out. Daisy giggled and Dessie joined in.

'Well! At least there is some hope you two won't be going around with long sad Mulhern faces all the time,' said Dottie, looking in at their smiling faces. 'I suppose that at least is something to be thankful for!'

The First Visitors

The first visitors to arrive were Bill Mulhern and two very strange little girls. They were neither pretty nor ugly – just a bit different! They looked alike, although one was smaller than the other. Their hair was a dirty blonde colour and was tied back in pigtails. These pigtails shot out at right angles to their ears. There was a generous sprinkling of freckles all over their faces.

'Aren't you going to kiss the twins then?' invited Bill Mulhern as Gertie and

Nellie Mulhern stood looking in at their brand new brother and sister.

'How come no one thinks to ask us if we want to be kissed?' hissed Dessie in anger across to Daisy. 'I can't say that I want those two slobbering all over me.'

'You would think they were talking to each other,' remarked Bill. 'They look to be two very clever babies.' The twins brightened immediately on hearing that remark but then heard 'Yuck! Crabbit looking little sods, that's what I think'. It was the younger of the two girls who was about nine years old. She leaned down and gave a quick peck on the cheek to each twin in turn as though they suffered from a terrible disease.

'Stop taking over the whole place!' hissed the older one, whom the twins later found out was Gertie. She pushed Nellie to one side and stood looking at them in horror.

'Gosh! They haven't one hair on their heads. We will be the laughing stock of the place. I told you, you were too old to have babies,' and she pointed a finger accusingly at her mother. 'What will my friends say?' and she started to wail at the top of her voice.

'Hush, Gertie dear!' comforted their mother. 'We can hide them away for a few weeks until their hair grows.'

Daisy and Dessie at this stage felt so humiliated and ashamed, they wished the ground would swallow them up.

'Two ill mannered little creeps,' fumed Daisy in anger.

'It's not as if they are great beauties themselves,' thought Dessie in fury. He peered out at them from his crib. He was fascinated by their pigtails that seemed to stick out at an odd angle above their ears.

'There is no need for that,' interrupted Bill Mulhern. 'Your mum has had a tough time these past few days. I think you did a very good job Dottie dear,' and he leaned forward and kissed Dottie on the cheek. 'I think the twins are just lovely.'

At last! Someone admired them. Daisy

and Dessie brightened up again immediately. Two big smiles lit up their faces. Their dad wasn't such a bad chap after all. But then he had to go and spoil it all with a sick joke.

'We can call them "the eggheads",' he spluttered. He thought this was hilarious. He started to laugh until the tears rolled down his cheeks. This in turn brought on a wheezing attack. He took out his inhaler.

The twins looked at him with disgust.

For the remainder of visiting time the twins were ignored for the most part. Gertie and Nellie were too busy stuffing themselves with the goodies that their dad had brought for their mum, and Bill and Dottie were sitting on the edge of the bed looking through a book called 'Baby Names'. The twins dozed off and were glad to see that the visitors had gone when they woke up.

That evening, as the twins lay in the nursery chatting in baby language to 'Ginger', 'Hairy' and 'Baldy', a group of strange looking visitors swarmed in. The hospital notice clearly said 'NO VISITING AFTER 6PM' but this lot didn't care.

'Where are they? Can we see them?' the twins could hear in the distance. There was no nurse around. Dessie peered out of his crib with fright. 'I wonder who they are looking for?'

A small bony lady spotted him.

'There they are – two little angels!'

she shrieked.

'Angels?' Daisy was curious. 'Where?' She tried to peer out but couldn't see any angels. 'Adults are very strange', she thought, but this lot were stranger than most. There was a very loud lady who was prodding Dessie with her long painted nail.

'Isn't he sweet?' she remarked. 'Couldn't you just eat him up?' Pure fright showed on Dessie's face. He was going to be eaten! He tried to make himself as small as possible. There was a fatter baby in the next crib. With a bit of luck she might go for him instead. Then it was Daisy's turn.

'I wonder which of the two is the little girl?' asked the silly looking man with her. As he leaned over, his hair moved on his head and Daisy was terrified that it was going to drop down on top of her. Dessie was looking over in disgust.

'Imagine not knowing that he was the boy and Daisy the girl? How thick can you get?' Then it was the small bony lady's turn.

'This is your granny Mulhern,' said the silly looking man with the hairpiece, as he pointed the slim, wiry-looking woman out to twins. In the meantime Granny was polishing her little round spectacles. Then she peered into each crib in turn.

'I can see them properly now. Sickly looking little devils,' she whispered to the others as she looked around to make sure no one else could hear. 'Not exactly oil paintings are they? They take after her side – those Brownes always look sickly. I mean, look at the two white faces of them. No! They will never have a day's health! Why our Bill had to go and marry that one is beyond me!' With these words granny poked and prodded them before fixing their baby blankets snugly around them.

This conversation was above the heads of the twins. They didn't understand. All they knew was that they were two sickly looking little bald twins and that no one could tell which was male or female. Nobody wanted them. They would be unwell all their lives and they would only have a birthday every four years. Charming! The future indeed looked bleak.

Thankfully one of the kind nurses ran in and rescued them.

'Can you not read the sign that says 'no visitors allowed?' she asked, quite crossly. Daisy could plainly see the little cheeky boy who was with them stick out his tongue behind the nurse's back. She was to find out later that he was her cousin David, son of the couple who were with him, namely her aunt Norma and uncle Mervyn – a right little horror!

'Our relatives seem to be a very common lot,' hissed Dessie to Daisy as the nurse ushered them out of the nursery. Ginger overheard him from the next crib.

'You can say that again,' said Ginger. I'd hate to have relatives like that.

The Twins are Named

Next morning a nurse arrived in, walked over to 'Baldy's crib and pinned a card to the top end of it. The card read 'Megan Marie'.

'There you are Megan Marie,' said the nurse cheerfully. 'I hope that you like your new name and I also have a name card here that says "Malcolm Edward Charles". She walked to Ginger's crib and pinned that name card on to it.

The twins envied Baldy and Ginger. What beautiful names! I wonder what our names will be, thought Daisy.

'Looks like you lot will have to wait another day or two for your names,' she added, smiling at the other babies. Then they were wheeled out to the wards again to begin a new day. Dottie seemed to be in a much brighter mood.

'My word, I do believe you two are putting on weight already. Your granny and granda Browne are coming today with your Aunt Lottie and Uncle Joe. You will have to be on your best behaviour.'

Then she began to hum as she began to feed and change the twins. The humming grated on the twins ears. All too soon it was visiting time. Granny and granda Browne arrived carrying two teddy bears followed by Aunt Lottie and Uncle Joe. There was no mistaking Lottie. She looked identical to Dottie her sister.

'So this is my little grandson?' said Granda Browne, looking at Dessie with interest. Then he glanced at Daisy and ignored her. 'It will be nice for Bill to have a son at last and for me to have a grand-

26

son,' he said proudly.

'Oh, great! thought Daisy. 'Welcome into our family Daisy Mulhern!'

'Where's the teddy then? Where's the teddy?' continued Granda, waving a teddy at Dessie.

'Can you believe this?' asked Dessie of Daisy. 'It's in your hand, stupid!' he replied with disgust.

Granny Browne had moved around to Daisy's cot.

'And how is my little tootsie wootsie?' she smiled, tickling Daisy's toes.

'Do you suppose there might be some little thing wrong with her upstairs?' enquired Daisy of Dessie. 'It seems like very strange language for an adult?'

Then it was Lottie's turn. A great wet kiss was planted on each twin's forehead and then she took out a camera and took photographs of the two of them.

'You are a very clever girl!' she gushed to Dottie. 'Imagine bringing these two into the world all by yourself.'

27

'But she had lots of help,' Daisy felt like saying but couldn't form the words.

Uncle Joe was the only visitor that the twins liked instantly.

'It must be nice to have a family,' he said to Dottie, 'especially two lively little twins like those. Congratulations!' and he shook her hand.

'If you want them you can keep them,' replied Dottie, sounding as if she meant it.

'Have you chosen names yet?' asked Lottie. 'Maybe we can help you.'

'We are leaving that to the two girls,' replied Dottie. The twins panicked. Imagine something as important as their names being left to their two airhead sisters! The twins were in despair.

Lottie turned out to be just as loud as her sister and with the same dress sense. She was wearing a green polka dot suit and purple dangly earrings. Just then the ward door opened and in walked 'Ginger's mum and dad with his dad, carrying 'Ginger' or rather, Malcolm Edward Charles.

'You must forgive us,' said Malcolm's dad, 'but we are so proud of our son Malcolm Edward – we feel that we must show him off to the world'.

'Yes!' said the tall, elegant lady in the cosy dressing gown. 'We waited a long time for this day. Congratulations by the way on your beautiful twins. Perhaps we can have you around to Malcolm Edward's christening party?'

Daisy wished the ground would open and swallow her. There was a complete contrast between the two families. Dottie's mouth was smeared with thick red lipstick as was Lottie's. Everything about them was coarse and vulgar. Malcolm's parents, on the other hand, were well mannered and refined. Daisy thought she could see a look of triumph on Malcolm's face.

'Lucky little sod,' Daisy thought. 'I wish we could change places.'

Dessie was thinking the exact same thing. The twins could hardly wait for visiting time to be over to get back to the nursery, partly to escape the Mulherns, and to get some sleep.

Next morning one of the friendly nurses arrived in as usual. She was carrying one name card. She pinned it onto Hairy's cot.

'There you are Lauren Rose! What a lovely name!'

Daisy had to agree. She would just love to have a name like that. She wondered what her's would be. She didn't have long to wait.

Once the babies were fed and changed the ward door opened and in ran Gertie and Nellie, shrieking at the top of their voices. They were closely followed by Dad Bill.

'No let me, let me,' shrieked Nellie as she arrived first and pinned two notices on the twins cots. Then she stood back in triumph and read aloud, 'Daisy and Dessie Mulhern'. Poor Dessie almost choked on his soother.

'What lovely names!' said Dottie.

'I chose Daisy,' said Gertie proudly, 'and Nellie chose Dessie because she fancies a little pimply geezer at school called "Desmond".'

'Get a grip on yourself Dessie,' he

thought. 'You can't let this get to you. These people are not normal. Maybe you can change it when you grow older?' He clenched his little baby fists in anger.

Meanwhile, Daisy had given up. She sobbed quietly into her pillow. A name said a lot about a person. She and her twin were now two little ugly bald babies, with horrid names whom nobody loved.

'Look!' shouted Gertie, 'I want to show you these.' From her bag she pulled out two pink bonnets. 'Now no one will know they are bald,' she added, as she plonked them on the babies' heads.

'Oh no! The shame of it,' thought Dessie – a pink bonnet on a boy!

As if she knew what he was thinking she added, 'I know pink is more for a girl but I thought two matching ones would be nicer seeing they are twins.'

Just then there was a brilliant flash that made the twins jump in their cots. Dad Bill was pressing a button on a little black box.

'This will be a very good photograph,' he

said to the twins. Then, as if he knew what Dessie was thinking, he said, 'Don't worry old boy! Pink suits you,' and he started to laugh.

When they were wheeled back to the ward the two nurses hooted with laughter when they saw the two name cards.

'Only the Mulherns could think of names like those,' laughed one of the nurses. 'I'm sorry to see these poor helpless babies go home to that Mulhern house tomorrow!'

'Not half as sorry as we are,' thought Daisy, in despair.

The Twins go Home

Next morning, the twins were brought into the ward bright and early.

'This is it!' said the nurse, cheerfully, as she wheeled them along the corridor. 'You are going home today.'

Dottie was already up and packing some of her things. She quickly fed and changed the babies.

'Your dad is arriving at 2pm,' she said to the twins. 'Probably will be late as usual. I hope the girls got that box room ready for you.'

'What's a box room?' whispered Daisy in

fright. 'Are they going to put us in boxes?'

'How should I know?' answered Dessie. 'Nothing would surprise me.' They lay, thinking the same thoughts.

'Malcolm Edward' was going home today as well. He had overheard his parents' talk about their plans for his homecoming. There was a special nursery designed for him that was full of toys. He would have a full-time nurse to look after his every need. His house had a large swimming pool, whatever that was?

Tears filled the babies' eyes. Life was so unfair. Megan Marie had already gone home with her large, happy family the day before and 'Lauren Rose' would not be going home until tomorrow but at least she was going home to a family who loved her and had a respectable home.

At three o'clock Bill arrived. He was out of breath.

'Sorry I'm late,' he said to Dottie as he kissed her on the cheek. 'The girls are planning a bit of a party.' Then he looked at the twins with the two pink bonnets pushed down over their ears. 'Do you know, son,' he asked Dessie, laughing, 'pink really does suit you?'

'Oh, yeah!' thought Dessie. 'How would you like a pink bonnet stuffed down on top of your bald skull?' As he thought this he giggled, and so did Daisy.

They might as well laugh as cry. They were on their way home to begin life with the Mulherns and there was nothing they could do about it.

Two nurses carried the twins to the car at the front door of the hospital. A large silver Mercedes was parked at the front entrance and a man whom the nurses called a chauffeur was standing holding the door open. Malcolm's mum was sitting in the back seat and the nurse was carefully handing Malcolm to her. He spotted the twins.

'Bye twins,' he shouted in baby language. 'It was nice knowing you!'

Further over stood an old rusty clapper

of a red car, all covered with decorations and balloons.

'That will be our transport,' whispered Dessie to Daisy, and he was right.

'The shame of it!' thought Daisy. Dottie pushed herself into the front seat. 'No, no!' exclaimed the nurse, 'you must sit in the back. It is too dangerous for the twins.'

'Twins! That's all I hear,' shrieked Dottie. 'Does anyone ever stop to think what Dottie wants? Oh! no! If those twins think that I am going to arrange my whole life around them then they are mistaken.'

The kind nurse looked taken aback by the outburst. However, after some per-suasion, Dottie agreed to sit in the back and the nurses placed the carrycots beside her in the seat.

Before the door closed they were just in time to see the silver Mercedes drive out the hospital entrance, carrying their little friend Malcolm to his new home.

As the car carrying the twins drove

through busy streets the twins could see nothing except their mum, painting her face in a small mirror.

'We will soon be there now,' said dad Bill, as he swung the car around the corner. The twins could hear loud music in the distance. 'That will be the girls ghetto-blaster,' continued Bill. 'The party is just beginning!'

Suddenly the car stopped. The car door opened. A large banner read 'Welcome home, Daisy and Dessie'. Of course, the twins could not read the banner but they could see words written in large letters across the banner.

A sea of faces peered in at the children. There were excited voices. Bill took one carrycot and Dottie the other.

This was the twins' first view of Duckweed Lane and their new home. Along the two sides of the road were rows of neatly painted houses and tidy gardens. Then, sticking out like a sore thumb, stood the house in front of them. It was painted yellow and purple with a lilac door. The fence around it was all broken and the long grass was covered with litter. The gate was half off.

Gathered around the house were lots of people but mainly children. Large balloons decorated the whole place and loud music was playing on a strange machine.

Then suddenly a huge hairy thing on four legs came charging at them and jumped up on Dottie and Bill. The twins

were terrified.

'Good dog, Caspar!' said Bill patting him on the head.

The twins screamed in pure terror.

'Let the little mites through,' shouted a kind woman at the back.

'They are frightened of that dog.'

She cleared a way for Dottie and Bill to get up the path. A smell of burning food was coming from the back of the house. Nellie suddenly appeared with black streaks all over her face. She was wailing at the top of her voice.

'The barbecue has gone on fire,' she shouted. 'The sausages are all burnt – help me someone!'

And so the twins were welcomed home to Duckweed Lane in a flurry of strange voices, black smoke and loud music!

During the next few hours the twins had to endure being poked and prodded by all sorts of strange people. Several adults lifted them and spoke in a strange language like 'coochie woochie woo!' and 'babesie wabesie' and so on. The twins couldn't understood whether these people were in some way handicapped or were they perhaps clever people who could speak several languages? Going by what they already knew of the Mulherns and the type of people they had as friends they thought that the handicap guess was probably the right one.

Later in the evening when the noise had died down and the friends had gone home, Bill lifted the two carrycots from the settee in the sitting room and said cheerfully, 'Have I got a surprise for you two? Gertie and Nellie have been getting your room ready. Come and see.'

Bill carried the babies upstairs, followed by Gertie and Nellie. Dottie said she would look at the room later because her feet were killing her but the twins saw her stifle a yawn, as if it was all too much bother.

Bill opened the door and the sickly smell of new paint almost made the twins vomit. Their eyes were dazzled for a few minutes until they got used to the brightness. A luminous green paint covered the walls. Two cots stood side by side with a mat between. On the mat was a monster's face with one eye and an evil grin. Strange mobiles hung from the ceiling. The babies suddenly longed for the cosy nursery and the life they had left behind.

It was then they noticed it. On the far wall and looking straight over at their twin cots was a large family photograph. At the back stood Dottie and Bill with Nellie and Gertie standing in front. They all looked as if they had come straight out of a horror movie!

The two girls lifted a twin each and put them in their cots. The smell of cheap paint was overpowering. Bill tucked them in.

'Aren't we supposed to sing them to sleep?' asked Nellie. 'That's what they do in films.'

'Please yourselves,' replied Bill, 'as long as you don't ask me to listen. I am going downstairs for a cup of tea.'

He left the room and Gertie also went

out but was soon back carrying a large instrument.

'I will play the guitar and you can sing,' she said to Nellie.

The twins could not believe their ears when they heard the loud wail that came out of Nellie's mouth. Gertie meanwhile was making terrible screeching noises with the guitar.

'How long do you suppose they will keep this up?' asked Daisy of Dessie.

'They won't stop until we sleep,' he hissed across, urgently. 'Close your eyes and pretend you are asleep. It is the only way we will get rid of them.'

Daisy did as her brother asked and sure enough, Gertie and Nellie sneaked out of the room, although why they were sneaking the twins could not understand, as the noise they had been making before that would have woken the dead.

The twins then began to discuss their fate. This was serious. How would they ever survive on Duckweed Lane?

They could imagine Malcolm gurgling in his baby chair with a kind nurse at this side. They could see Megan playing happily with her family and, Lauren sleeping peacefully in the nursery.

All of a sudden a large monster's face with an evil eye was looking at Daisy. She screamed aloud and no one came. She woke up and peered over at Dessie in the cot beside her.

'Gosh, Daisy! You frightened the life and out of me!' exclaimed Dessie.

'I wish I was back in the nursery,' cried Daisy.

'So do I,' replied Dessie. They both cried but no one came to comfort them. It was a good while before the twins drifted off again into an uneasy sleep in their new home.

The Twins Settle In

Next morning the twins awoke and their tummies were rumbling with hunger. The two babies started to bawl. It seemed an age before their dad arrived to bring them downstairs. Gertie and Nellie were already up and dressed in two matching outfits. They were each carrying a bag of books. They hardly looked at the twins, as they seemed to be in a rush.

'Look at the time,' said Gertie. 'We will be late for school. We had better fly.'

'Pity we can't see out the window,' thought

Dessie, as the door slammed behind them. 'I would love to see those two fly!'

Bill got the twins their bottles and then changed them.

'We will give your mum a little rest today,' he said. 'Granny Mulhern will call around later.'

Later, as their dad opened the back door, the large hairy mutt that they had seen the previous day came bounding into the kitchen.

'Sit Caspar! Sit!' shouted their dad, but the dog ran over and looked in at the twins in their carrycots. Dessie and Daisy both wet themselves with fright and they started to bawl.

'Now look what you've done!' shouted Bill to Caspar, as he caught him and hauled him out into the garden.

'Do you suppose he would eat us?' asked Daisy with fright, in her baby language.

Dessie was too frightened to reply. He just lay there wondering what kind of strange house this was. Just then, Dottie arrived from upstairs. As usual, she looked like something from a horror movie. Her head was covered with rollers.

'Hope you two are behaving yourselves?' she asked the twins, as she passed by in a cloud of smoke.

'You know what the nurse said about smoking in

  the same room as the babies,' said their father.

'Oh, not you and all!' replied Dottie. 'Do you want to make two proper wallies of them? We need to toughen them up'.

Then, she plonked herself on the sofa and turned on a strange box in the corner that the twins had seen in the hospital. 'Be a dear and get me a cuppa,' she said to Bill.

She sat back and watched the screen in front of her, ignoring the twins, as clouds of smoke rose around her.

A knock came to the front door and Dottie peered through the net curtain.

'That's just all I need,' she complained. 'Has that battle axe no home of her own?'

With great effort she opened the door.

'How lovely to see you gran,' she lied, as granny Mulhern walked in past her, laden down with two bags.

'I have decided to come and stay for a few weeks until you get your strength back. You are going to need all the help you can get with those two over there,' and she pointed in the direction of the twins.

'That's great, that is,' whispered Dessie. 'Talk about sending someone on a guilt trip.'

Daisy smiled. Sometimes Dessie could take offence very easily. Meanwhile she noticed Dottie making strange faces at her dad behind Granny Mulhern's back. She was sure Dottie was trying to say 'Get that one out of here!'

However, Granny Mulhern nattered on.

'What have I got here? Let's see now. I have nice matinée coats for those two that I knitted myself.' She took these from one of the bags. Then she continued. 'I brought some extra nappies. You will need those and I also have some things from the chemist.'

She was still nattering when Daisy dozed off into a deep sleep. She awoke to the sound of loud music from upstairs. 'Turn that racket down,' shouted Dottie. 'You will wake the twins.'

She seemed to forget that her own shouts would wake the dead. Little granny Mulhern was running around in a frilly apron setting the table. Bill was lying in an armchair and like the twins, had just woken up.

Gertie and Nellie came downstairs. Their clothes were untidy and their hair tousled.

'What happened to the two of you?' asked Dottie in alarm.

'We were in a fight at school today with Spice Malone and Mags Casey,' said Nellie. 'They said our twins were two ugly looking little warts. They won't be saying it again, that's for sure,' said Gertie.

'What's a wart?' asked Daisy of Dessie in baby language?

'How would I know?' whispered back Dessie.

'Isn't that sweet, Bill? Our two girls standing up for the twins.'

Dessie and Daisy felt a warm glow inside them. It was nice of Gertie and Nellie to stand up for them. They smiled across at each other. Maybe life with the Mulherns wouldn't be so bad after all.

Dottie Takes a Break

A few days later Dottie announced at breakfast that she needed a break and that was going off to stay with her sister, Lottie, for a week. 'Now that Granny Mulhern is here and you are taking a few weeks off work, it is a good chance for me to get a break,' she told Bill.

'You and Granny Mulhern will manage fine and it will do me the world of good,' she said to Bill.

'It just wasn't natural,' thought Dessie from his cot in the corner. 'Imagine a mother deserting her babies at that important stage of life when they were supposed to bond with her.'

Daisy sucked on her soother. She could hardly believe what she was hearing. Her mum was deserting her at a very important time of her life.

However, Bill seemed glad to see Dottie go. He helped her to pack her things and spent the day whistling cheerfully.

When Aunt Lottie arrived that evening and took Dottie with her in the car the twins were sure they saw Bill Mulhern do a little jig in the kitchen and rub his hands with glee.

That evening Aunt Norma, Uncle Mervyn and cousin David arrived. David went to look at the twins. Dessie and Daisy didn't feel comfortable when he was near them.

'I know,' he said to Gertie and Nellie, excitedly, 'why don't you have their ears pierced? They would look really cool.'

Gertie looked to be taken with the idea 'David you are a genius!' she replied.

'Why didn't we think of that?'

'I'm not sure that I'm too keen on that idea,' mused Nellie. 'Aren't they a bit young for that sort of thing?'

'I never heard such nonsense,' replied the older sister. 'Just think! The bonny baby show will be on soon. Those two haven't a hope with those two bald heads unless we help them out.'

'I agree,' said David. 'We could call

them "the twins with attitude!"'

'Oh yeah! That would really swing it with the judges,' replied Nellie, sarcastically.

Already the twins could see clearly that Nellie appeared to be the brighter of the two sisters.

'The cheek of them,' muttered Dessie in his baby language. 'Haven't a hope indeed! Well, we will show them!'

'It's alright for you,' hissed Daisy 'you're a boy. Boys are sometimes bald, but girls!' Her lip quivered and tears stung the back of her two little eyes. She started to bawl.

'Now look what you've all done,' screeched Granny Mulhern from the kitchen. 'Go on, clear off and leave the twins alone.'

Granny came in and chased the three children upstairs. The twins were glad when the visitors had gone and Gertie and Nellie were busy upstairs with their homework. They watched as Bill prepared their evening feed. He was cheerfully whistling to himself as he spooned the milk powder into the bottles.

'Don't know what you are so cheerful about?' remarked Granny as she fussed around tidying cushions and wiping the table. 'Your wife has just left you on your own. You have two squawling babies to look after, not to mention two ill-mannered little so-and-sos upstairs and you decide to whistle. You can put any ideas of going up to the bookies to bet on horses out of your head. And as for the pub?'

'You worry too much! That's your problem Mum, let's face it. Dottie is not exactly your favourite person to be around. Besides, it is like old times. Just you and me,' he hesitated, 'and the kids, of course! You and I will make a great team'.

He leaned over and gave her a hug. Granny looked pleased. 'Now Mum! If you feed the twins, I will make the two of us a nice cup of tea. Then you can put your feet up while I clear the dishes.'

'Well! If you are sure,' answered Granny

looking doubtful. 'I must say it is a bit like old times, just you and me together.

Then she fed the twins in turn, changed them and tucked them in.

'Goodnight my lovelies,' she whispered to them. 'Pleasant dreams!' She switched out the light and left the room.

'Why was Bill Mulhern in such good humour since their mum had gone to stay with Aunt Lottie?' wondered Daisy, in the dark.

When she asked Dessie he whispered, 'Think about it. If you were stuck with Dottie Mulhern and someone came to take her away wouldn't you be in good humour too?'

Daisy had to agree.

Life with Granny Mulhern

The twins awoke to the most awful roar coming from downstairs.

'Tight fisted old hag!' was what they could plainly hear Nellie say as she and Gertie slammed the front door.

'Did you hear that Bill?' asked Granny. 'Just because I wouldn't give them any extra money along with the bus fare. That is what is wrong with young ones these days. Too much money and not enough respect for their elders!'

The twins smiled to themselves.

'Serves Gertie and Nellie right!' they thought. Already the twins had figured that Granny Mulhern was a tough little lady who lay down the law.

Soon they were brought downstairs and were fed and changed.

'What boring lives we babies have,' whispered Dessie to Daisy. 'I could do with some excitement. There must be more to life than this!'

'What do you mean?' enquired Daisy. Sometimes she worried about this strange twin of her's. He seemed to be more intelligent than the average baby. What she didn't realise was that both twins had been born with above average intelligence and this would make for an exciting life in the years ahead.

As it happened, Dessie didn't have long to wait for some excitement. After breakfast Granny did a very strange thing. She put her hand in her mouth and pulled out her teeth. She left them on the coffee table while she went off out to the kitchen.

'How did she do that?' asked Daisy.

'I expect everyone can do that,' thought Dessie, although he wasn't too sure.

Just then, Caspar the dog came in the open back door. He ran into the room, lifted Granny's teeth in this mouth and ran out the door again. When granny came back she couldn't find her teeth. She searched high and low and when Bill came back from the shop she was almost in tears.

'I know I left them on the coffee table,' she explained.

'Look, Mum,' said Bill gently. 'You're not as young as you used to be. Now think again.'

Dessie and Daisy both tried to explain in baby language where the teeth had gone to no avail.

'You would almost think those twins are trying to tell me something,' she said.

Dad explained to Gertie and Nellie when they came home why Granny was so upset.

'Serves her right,' said Gertie. 'I hope

58

she doesn't expect us to help her look for them.'

'I will help you to look for them if you pay me well,' replied Nellie, cheekily. Granny ignored that remark.

The problem was solved half an hour later when Bill went out to feed Caspar and found the teeth in the doghouse.

'That will teach her to keep her clappers in her mouth,' hissed Nellie.

The twins felt sorry for Granny and they had to agree with her when she spoke to Bill later in the evening after the girls had gone out.

'Two right nasty little pieces of work, those two. Take after the Brownes if you ask me!' Bill, however, was sitting watching the box in the corner where a large group of men were running around after a ball. He was so taken with what these men were doing that he didn't seem to hear Granny.

Daisy and Dessie thought these men looked ridiculous chasing a silly little ball and at their age. Daisy wondered if all men were perhaps a little silly but she didn't dare say so to Dessie. After all, he was a boy and she didn't want to hurt his feelings.

The next crisis to hit the family concerned Daisy and Dessie themselves. They hadn't got proper nappies like the lovely soft ones the nurses in the hospital had told them to get. The twins had clearly heard Dottie say she was not going to waste good Bingo money on expensive nappies for those two twirps!

Now, the twins bottoms began to feel sore. Daisy was too embarrassed at first to mention it to Dessie because there are some things a girl keeps secret but not so in the Mulhern house. When Bill was changing their nappies that Friday evening Gertie exclaimed, 'Oh, look! Their bottoms are all red!' Then she and Nellie went into hoots of laughter. Poor Dessie went all pink.

'Let me see?' said Granny Mulhern, as she too came up to look.

'Feel free,' thought Dessie in disgust. 'Why don't we call in the whole neighbourhood. Look everyone! Dessie and Daisy's bottoms are on show!'

'Leave them to me,' said Granny.

Now that the fun was over the two girls went off to the sitting room. Granny went to the bathroom and came back a short time later with a large jar of cream.

'This should do the trick,' she said, as she rubbed in a large dollop into each twins bottom. Then she replaced the nappies again.

Daisy could feel a strange burning sensation as could Dessie. After a few minutes Daisy felt as if she was on fire. Dessie felt the same. Both twins started to scream.

Gertie and Nellie even came running from the sitting room.

'Whatever is the matter?' asked Bill. 'Maybe those nappies are too tight!' When he took them off he asked Granny, 'What cream did you use?'

'Baby cream,' she replied 'At least I think it was. I couldn't find my spectacles to read the writing. Here it is.' She lifted the jar of cream from the floor and the two girls went into hysterics laughing.

'It says "Jif Cleansing Cream" on the jar,' hooted Nellie. Granny looked at the twins in horror.

'Oh, you poor little mites,' she said. 'Quickly Bill! Carry them into the bathroom.' The first relief the twins got was when the cool refreshing water from the shower soothed the soreness. Gertie and Nellie found it all very funny.

'I wonder how they would feel if their bottoms were on fire?' wondered Daisy.

Granny meanwhile put on the proper cream and the twins got some relief. However, it was late into the night before either of them got a wink of sleep, such was the pain they felt.

The twins were very cranky next day because they were still sore.

'Oh, shut up, the pair of you,' shouted

Nellie. 'Don't be such wimps.'

The twins bawled all the louder. Even Granny Mulhern and their dad left them in the kitchen and went off into the sitting room and shut the door firmly behind them.

'What now?' sniffed Daisy. 'No one is paying any attention to us.'

'The important thing,' replied Dessie 'is never give up. Come on! Give it all you've got.'

Both twins opened their mouths and bawled. Their dad was the first out, followed by Granny Mulhern. Dessie peeped out to see how they were affected. After all, Daisy and he deserved a little more sympathy than what they were getting.

'What are we going to do with them?' asked Bill.

'Leave that to me,' said Granny. She went over to the cupboard and took out a very old bottle that had the words 'Herbal Remedy' written on it.

'You surely aren't going to give them that?' enquired Bill, remembering how Gran used to give his brother Cedric and

himself doses of it as children. 'It would tear strips off the wallpaper', his Dad Jack used to joke back then. This stuff wasn't something to joke about though. Bill could hardly wait to see the twins' reaction.

Gran got two bottles and put a large spoonful of the liquid in each bottle with sugar and warm water. The twins watched fascinated. Then she forced the warm, sickly liquid down the twins' throats. It felt like rocket fuel. The twins began to feel strangely 'woozy'.

'There, that will do the trick,' she remarked. 'I reared you and Ceddy on that stuff.'

'What exactly is in it?' asked Bill. 'I still get tears in my eyes even thinking about it.'

'It is a herbal mix which my granny passed on to me. It is great stuff for putting babies to sleep. Now, I will make a nice cup of tea for each of us to calm the nerves. Those two would try the patience of a saint!'

The twins ignored the remark and dozed off into a peaceful, restful sleep.

They awoke to the sound of the phone ringing. It was Dottie. They could hear Granny Mulhern remark to their dad afterwards.

'Huh! Took her time ringing.'

The Twins' First Outing

'It would do those twins the world of good if they were to get some fresh air,' remarked Granny Mulhern. 'I think it is time to bring them for a walk.

She took in the brand new twin pram that Uncle Joe and Aunt Lottie had bought the twins as a present and started to get the twins ready.

'I hope she doesn't put on that silly looking pink bonnet,' whispered Dessie to Daisy, but it was the first thing she put on. When both twins were lying side by side in the pram she stood back to admire them.

'I just wish your Grandpa Jack were alive to see you both,' she said, smiling.

On their way down the street several people came over to talk to Granny and to look at the twins. Dessie was feeling uncomfortable.

'A pink bonnet on a boy! Have these people no sense?'

He didn't feel any better when several people mistook them both for girls. His face went a bright red each time someone looked in the pram and remarked, 'Oh! Two beautiful little girls!'

When they reached what granny called 'The shop' she went inside leaving the twins outside the door. A group of cheeky children came over and began to make faces at them. Some were frightening and the twins started to cry.

'Cry babies!' shouted one child.

'Keep your hair on!' shouted another.

'They don't have any hair,' laughed another.

The twins were glad when Granny came out and chased them away.

The next person who stopped and spoke to Granny was a man dressed in a dark suit, with a white collar whom Granny called 'Your Reverence'. He spoke about a 'christening' day and used other big words that the twins didn't understand.

'What are your names my little poppets!' he asked.

'What is a poppet?' asked Dessie and Daisy.

'I haven't a clue,' whispered Daisy in her baby language.

'Oh! Listen to that lively baby gurgling,' said the Reverend.

'Their names are Daisy and Dessie,' said Granny. The twins thought they could see the flicker of a smile hover around the Reverend's mouth.

'How very unusual,' he remarked. 'Yes, very unusual indeed.'

'It wasn't my idea,' continued Granny. No, I would have chosen ... let's see now!

Yes! – Borris and Bertha after my Uncle Boris and I always liked the name Bertha.'

Granny nattered on and the twins could definitely see the Reverend yawn.

'Lucky for us that she didn't get to choose our names,' whispered Daisy.

'I will call up to the house next week to arrange the christening,' said the Reverend as he said goodbye.

'That will do,' replied Granny. 'Dottie, their mum will be home by then.'

The Reverend did not look impressed.

'Dottie! I see!' As he walked off into the distance the twins could near him repeat, 'Daisy, Dessie and Dottie – Daisy, Dessie and Dottie! Oh dear! What a tongue twister!'

'Nice man!' muttered Granny as she pushed the twins' pram towards home.

Up ahead was a shop with a sign that read 'Butcher' over the door. Granny stopped the pram outside the shop.

'Just nipping in here a few minutes,' she said to the twins, 'to get a few chops for the tea.' No sooner had she gone in than up came Gertie and Nellie with a few of their pals to the pram.

'Look!' said Nellie, 'Granny has left the twins outside. Doesn't she know that babies can be kidnapped? You take Daisy and I'll take Dessie.'

The twins couldn't believe their ears.

'When she comes out she will panic. Serves her right for leaving them outside!'

Daisy and Dessie were lifted from the pram and Nellie and Gertie ran with them and hid behind some cars on the other side of the street.

'Look out!' shouted one of their pals. 'Here she comes!'

Granny Mulhern came out of the shop, let the brake off the pram and continued walking in the direction of the house.

'I don't believe this!' said Gertie, 'She doesn't realise they are missing.'

They ran up behind her and the twins could distinctly hear Granny muttering to herself.

'Nice man, that butcher. I got some lovely fat chops for our tea. It's a pity you two can't eat. Never mind. I will get your dad to get two nice bottles of milk ready for you.'

Soon she reached the house with the empty pram and took out her key.

'Blind old bat!' muttered Nellie. 'Our trick is spoiled.'

The twins smiled to themselves. They were beginning to bond with Granny Mulhern.

That was a nasty mean trick the girls

had played. Nellie and Gertie came up behind Granny on the step

'Aren't you forgetting something?' Nellie asked Granny in disgust. 'Gertie and I took the twins out of the pram at the butchers. You have been wheeling an empty pram the whole way home.'

'How thoughtful of you,' replied Granny, 'to let the twins get the full good of the fresh air. I think I may have been wrong about you two.'

The twins could see Gertie and Nellie look at each other in dismay. Their nasty prank was ruined. 'Ah well! It's good to be home,' continued Gran. 'I'll put the kettle on and you two can put the twins into their cots.'

The twins tittered to themselves. Good old Gran!

The Bonny Baby Show

Dottie Mulhern arrived home the following Monday. With her was Aunt Lottie and Granny and Grandpa Browne. Dottie looked different. She was a deep chocolate brown colour as was her sister Lottie. The twin sisters had identical hairstyles - short blonde hair with strange colours mixed in.

'Anyone would think that you two were abroad,' remarked Bill as he opened the front door to them.

'I'm glad you like it,' replied Dottie. 'We

were on the sunbeds.'

'I didn't hear him say he liked it,' whispered Daisy in her baby language.

'They look like two big brown teddies,' giggled Dessie. Aunt Lottie noticed him smiling.

'What is my little petal smiling at?' she asked. Dessie wondered what she meant. Then she called to Dottie.

'Do you know love? That baby is definitely a Browne. He has a nice pleasant temperament.'

'What does temperament mean?' whispered Dessie to Daisy.

'How should I know?' replied Daisy.

Grandpa Browne came over and lifted him from the pram.

'This little man will bowl all the ladies over in another few years. You mark my words!'

'I don't want to bowl anyone over,' thought Dessie. 'What can he mean at all?'

Granny Browne then picked up Daisy.

'Do you know, I cannot tell the difference

between them!'

'That is just great,' thought Daisy looking over at her little bald brother in his Grandpa's arms. Secretly she would have liked to be a little less like him. Meanwhile Dessie was looking across at Daisy and wishing he wasn't so like her. Then he felt guilty. After all, she was his twin and was definitely his best friend.

Dottie, as usual, didn't show any great interest in the newborns and, while the visitors chatted to them for a while, they soon got tired and left them back in their cots.

Bill left to take Granny Mulhern home. She had had a busy week and now that Dottie was home there was no need for her to stay around. The twins felt that Dottie was glad to see her go.

When the twins awoke later the house was quiet, as the visitors had gone. Bill was lying in an old armchair snoozing and Dottie was looking through a paper. Suddenly she shrieked.

'Look Bill! A Bonny Baby Competition in the Town Hall next Saturday. We will have to enter the twins for that!'

'What is a bonny baby competition?' wondered Daisy.

It didn't take long to find out. For the next few days the twins heard little else. Gertie and Nellie were making all the plans. They would rub fake tan on the babies to take 'the sickly white look off them.'

Nellie knew a boy at school called 'Fibber Lonergan' who knew of 'stuff' that could make a person's hair grow. They asked Dottie to allow them to get the twins' ears pierced and to put studs in them. Daisy and Dessie didn't know what that meant but they knew their ears were very sensitive parts of their bodies and they felt it wouldn't be a good idea. They hoped Dottie wouldn't agree.

'They are a bit young,' she said doubt-fully. 'It might not be wise.'

'How else do you expect them to win?'

sulked Gertie. 'Those two need all the help they can get.'

'Oh, thanks a lot,' hissed Dessie.

Dottie had her own ideas. She would buy them two nice matching suits and caps! She would give them extra feeds to take the thin, scrawny look off their skinny legs. She would allow a certain amount of fake tan but didn't think the hair growing lotion would be good for them as it might bring them out in a rash and that would spoil their chances altogether.

Finally the day of the Bonny Baby Show arrived. Daisy and Dessie were bathed, powdered and dressed in two matching striped suits with caps.

'They look like escaped convicts,' laughed Bill.

'I wish people would stop laughing at us,' whispered Daisy.

On the way to the Town Hall they passed lots of other prams all heading in the same direction. A ticket was pinned on each baby as they were wheeled through the door. The hall was packed with babies.

Somehow the twins felt that there was something not right about this type of thing. They felt like exhibits at a show.

Gertie and Nellie strutted up and down looking at the other babies and the twins could hear them plainly say out loud 'wasted little weed' or 'silly looking little runt' as they passed each baby in turn. Daisy and Dessie could feel their faces going red. Their two older sisters were a big embarrassment to them.

Meanwhile Dottie got talking to another mother and seemed to have forgotten all about the twins.

Gertie and Nellie lifted them from the pram.

'The judges will never see them in there,' said Nellie. Dessie could see baby Malcolm further up the hall with his proud mum and dad. Megan and Lauren Rose were there too with their parents, brothers and sisters.

Soon all the babies were lined up along

the wall.

A man came and whispered to Dottie that she was in the wrong place and that she would need to move further down the hall to the 'Twins Section'.

A few men and ladies walked about talking to the babies.

'Seems silly,' thought Daisy, 'talking to us babies when they know perfectly well that we can't speak their language.' Dessie agreed.

When Dottie reached the place marked 'Twins' she looked surprised to see that there were no other twins there. A man came over and pinned a large 'first' on their pram.

'It seems like you are the only twins here,' he said to Daisy and Dessie, 'so you have to come "first" in this section.' Then he shook hands with Dottie and congratulated her.

'Why?' wondered Daisy. 'She didn't win anything. Then again neither did we. We are the only ones here.'

Gertie and Nellie started to complain. Of all the mean rotten tricks! That means that they didn't have to go to all that bother. They would have won anyway!

The twins were embarrassed at their loud display.

A press photographer arrived to take photographs of the winning babies with their mums. Gertie and Nellie insisted on pushing their way in to the group as well.

As they left the hall Malcolm's pram passed by them.

'How are things with you two?' he asked smiling, 'I'm glad you won.'

'What a decent little chap Malcolm is,' thought Dessie.

Dottie was in great humour on the way home.

'Imagine! We will all be in the paper this week. You can go in to school tomorrow and tell that Spice Casey and Mags Malone that our "two ugly warts" got first prize in the Bonny Baby Show. Let us see baby Casey or baby Malone beat that!' she told Gertie and Nellie.

'Do you think it is wise dear to get involved in a kiddies' row?' asked Bill.

'What are you?' shrieked Dottie, 'a man or a mouse?'

'What does she mean?' wondered Dessie. 'Of course he is a man'.

It was all too confusing. He snuggled down beside Daisy and was soon fast asleep.

Malcolm's Christening

A few days later a letter arrived at the Mulhern house. Bill brought it into the kitchen and read part of it aloud.

An Invitation
The Mulhern family with the twins are invited to a party at Ashford Manor to celebrate the christening of Malcolm Edward Charles on this Saturday at 3 pm.
Signed:
Mr and Mrs Charles Kendrick

'Gosh!' said Dottie. 'Imagine those yuppies inviting us up to that posh "do"! Wait till they hear this down at Bingo! And all for that little snivelling git of a son of theirs.'

The twins smiled. They hoped Dottie and Bill would go. They had often wondered about Malcolm and the house he lived in. However, they began to change their minds later when they thought of how loud Dottie and their sisters were. Dottie had her mind made up though and there was no changing it.

'You will have to wear that nice new suit,' she said to Bill, 'and I will bring the girls shopping tomorrow. Oh, this is exciting!'

She went out into the hall to phone around and tell any of her neighbours who would care to listen.

As Gertie and Nellie began to prepare for Malcolm's christening party, the twins could only think of the Cinderella story which Bill had read for them a few times. That was the thing about this family. Even though the Cinderella story was much too difficult for them to understand, Bill went ahead and read it anyway. The twins supposed that in normal families parents probably read stories that suited the baby's age. However, they had figured that the stepmother and the two ugly sisters were probably very much like Dottie, Gertie and Daisy, and that the Ball was probably like a christening party. They laughed to themselves as Gertie and Nellie fought over every little thing, just like the ugly sisters in the book. Dottie tried to get them to wear dresses.

'I wouldn't be seen dead in a dress!' shouted Gertie.

'Neither would I!' added Nellie.

'Oh dear!' said Dottie. 'Bill will you talk to them?'

The two girls, however, marched out and slammed the door.

On another day Dottie told the girls 'Be sure and tell your friends at school that we are all invited up to Ashford Manor'.

'Why?' they wanted to know.

'Are you stupid or what?' shrieked Dottie.

The twins giggled as they knew the answer. 'Definitely stupid!' they whispered.

So the week passed with one argument after another. Finally Saturday arrived. The twins almost choked on their bottles when they saw the heavily painted Dottie coming downstairs in a bright red suit with a very short skirt.

'Are you still feeding those two?' she asked Bill. 'Hurry or we will be late!'

Next to arrive downstairs were Gertie and Nellie. They were dressed in matching orange dungarees and T-shirts. Their pigtails stuck out on each side at even odder angles than before.

'You look very nice,' lied Dottie. And, of course, the twins knew without being told that it was very wrong to tell lies.

'Now help me to get these two dressed,' she said, pointing at the twins as if they were two family pets. When the twins were dressed in their striped suits and matching caps, Bill arrived down. There was a ring on the doorbell.

'That will be the car around for us,' said Dottie. 'Now I don't want anyone shaming me in front of the McKendricks.'

'I wonder who will shame who?' thought Daisy as Dottie opened the door and outside stood a man in a dark suit with shiny buttons and a peaked cap. He lifted his cap and said 'If sir and madam are ready, then follow me.' At this Gertie and Nellie went into shrieks of laughter and began to point at his strange waistcoat, all the while whispering and giggling. It was only when Dottie looked at them crossly that they stopped.

The man, meanwhile, was holding the car door open for them to get in. He looked snootily at the two girls as they got into the car. The twins couldn't help noticing some of the neighbours standing outside in their gardens, looking in their direction.

'That is a feather out of their tails,' smirked Dottie, with satisfaction, looking over at them with glee.

'Whatever does she mean?' thought Dessie.

Daisy, meanwhile, remembered that this was the same man that had held the door open for Malcolm on the day he had left the hospital. The nurse had called him a chauffeur.

The large car sped through the streets and soon turned up into a huge drive with trees on each side. Ahead of them they could see a big house, a little like the castle in Bill's *Cinderella* book.

'Gosh! Look at the class house,' said Gertie, her eyes almost popping out of her head.

'Posh gits,' was Nellie's reply.

As they got nearer they saw there were

tables and chairs out on the lawn and a large tent that the chauffeur called a marquee standing to the side. Already people had arrived and there were several baby prams there as well. A few ladies dressed in black with white aprons seemed to be looking after the babies.

When the car stopped at the front door, Malcolm's mother came down the steps to meet them.

'You are all very welcome to Ashford Manor,' she smiled as she shook hands. 'Malcolm's christening was this morning but now we are having a little afternoon celebration. Charles and I want to see the babies that were born around the same time as him. We feel it is important to keep in touch.'

'What a lovely lady,' thought Daisy.

'Snob!' thought Gertie and Nellie.

Malcolm's mum led them down to the garden and introduced them to the other people there. All that the twins were interested in was meeting Malcolm, Megan and Lauren.

They wanted to hear all about their families and their homes, and to find out if the adults in their lives spoke in a strange language. Malcolm's mum told Dottie to leave the twins pram beside the other prams.

'The staff will look after them for you,' she said kindly.

The twins knew that Dottie was delighted to be free of them and they too were glad to be free of her. Meanwhile Gertie and Nellie were over at one of the tables doing what they could always do best – stuffing themselves with food.

The twins spent a very enjoyable afternoon at Ashford Manor. They heard about Malcolm's large house, all his toys, the swimming pool and his new pet dog.

Then it was Megan's turn. They laughed when they heard about all the animals that lived on her farm. Megan described the clucking of the hens, the grunt of the pigs and the lowing of the cows. Lauren was enjoying life with her older brother. He brought all his infant classmates home from school one day to show her off.

'It must be nice to be rich,' remarked Megan to Malcolm. 'Still, I wouldn't swop my family with anyone's. We don't have much money but we all love each other. That's what I think is important.'

'I think you are right,' Malcolm replied. The twins were surprised. 'In fact,' Malcolm continued, 'sometimes I wish my parents didn't have so much money. Then we could live in a smaller house. There would be no need for servants and my Mum could come and pick me up when I cry instead of my nurse.'

Malcolm's little eyes filled with tears and the twins felt sorry for him. Malcolm, with all his riches, was not as happy as they thought.

Lauren looked thoughtful. 'It is the feeling that you are loved that matters,' she gurgled, happily.

The twins wondered if anyone loved them. They felt lucky that they had each other and they knew too that Granny

Mulhern was on their side.

Then it was the twins' turn. They felt ashamed of their relatives but the babies all laughed heartily when they heard how Gertie and Nellie's trick went wrong and how the dog had gone off with Granny Mulhern's teeth. All too soon it was time for home. Dottie staggered over on her red high heel shoes and Bill told her she should not have drunk so much champagne.

Gertie and Nellie had a fight with some of Megan's brothers and sisters over a silly game of handball but apart from that they seemed to enjoy the day.

It was a very tired group who arrived home that evening in their chauffeur-driven car and two little tired twins slept in their new striped suits all through the night until eight o'clock the following morning.

When they awoke, it was to a loud screech from Dottie. Had anyone bothered to lock the garden gate the night before? Caspar was not in the garden. The gate was lying open. Caspar had gone missing.

Caspar Goes Missing

The twins wondered what all the fuss was about? After all, when Caspar was around they kept chasing him out of their way. Now that he was missing, there was major drama.

'He probably felt unloved like us,' whispered Daisy and Dessie. All of a sudden she felt sorry for Caspar. After all, she had Dessie. Caspar had no one.

'He did the right thing,' Dessie whispered back. 'I would run away too if I could.'

Gertie and Nellie cried all morning.

In the end Dottie could listen to them no longer. 'Aw, shut up! I have enough to put up with, what with listening to those two whingers in the corner.'

'I think she means us,' said Daisy, in alarm.

'Oh, you are very bright this morning,' replied Dessie.

Daisy felt hurt so she decided to sulk. She made up her mind that she would just lie there and think of poor Caspar some-where out there with no friends in the world except her.

A big search party got under way. Granny Mulhern Uncle Mervyn, Aunt Norma, David and Uncle Joe all called around, as did a few other people the twins didn't know. They heard Uncle Joe tell Dottie that Lottie had a headache and couldn't come.

'Too lazy, more like!' whispered Bill to Dottie.

'What will we do with those two?' asked

Gertie and Nellie, as they pointed accusingly in the twins' direction.

'I will take care of them,' replied
Granny Mulhern. 'I will go around the town
and put up notices in the shop windows.'

'A great idea Mum,' replied Bill. The
twins were glad to be with granny. She
seemed to be the only one in the whole
family with a few brains.

So the twins spent that afternoon
being wheeled around from shop to shop.
However, no one in the town had seen
Caspar.

There was more drama when they
arrived home. Dottie had just arrived in
before them and was covered in muck.

'She fell into a hole,' explained Uncle
Mervyn, who was with her. The twins were
sure they could see him laughing to himself. Dottie was in a very bad mood.

'Wait till that dog comes home! I will
wring his neck.'

'Whose neck will you wring?' asked the
tall gentleman dressed in black, who came

in the open hall door.

This was the man with the white collar who had talked about a 'christening'.

'Oh! It's you Reverend,' said Dottie.

'Who else?' whispered Dessie to Daisy and both started to giggle.

Granny took him in to the sitting room while Dottie went off to make herself, 'respectful', as she called it. All they could hear as she plonked upstairs was 'That mongrel of a dog', and 'Could that man not come when I look normal?'

'Then he would never come,' remarked Daisy, and the twins went into hoots of laughter.

After the Reverend had gone and the date of the christening was set, the others returned. All had the same story to tell. No one had seen Caspar. Gertie and Nellie began to howl again and Dottie chased them up to their room. Granny Mulhern and granny Browne made the tea while granda Browne sat beside Dessie's cot and spoke non-stop about fishing.

95

Dessie was glad when tea was ready.

'I am telling you Daisy,' remarked Dessie, 'one of these days I will flip. He keeps on about this large salmon that he and I will catch.'

'Whatever that is?' Daisy wondered as she smiled to herself.

The smell of the food reminded the twins that they hadn't had their bottles.

'Trust that lot to look after themselves first,' remarked Dessie. 'You would think the weakest in society should be seen to first'.

Daisy looked across at Dessie. Sometimes he surprised her with his deep thoughts.

'Let's remind them then!' she answered, and she and Dessie began to bawl as loud as they could.

'Oh no!' shouted Dottie. 'That's all we need.'

'Stay where you are everyone!' said Uncle Mervyn. 'That will be their teeth. I remember our David used to bawl like that too.'

'Not the brightest, is he?' asked Dessie.

'I wonder what he is going to do?'

It didn't take long for them to find out. Mervyn took out a tube of strange cream from their baby bag. The words 'Bonjela' were printed on the side. Then he squeezed some onto his large finger and stuck it into Daisy and Dessie's mouths in turn. The twins nearly choked.

'That is disgusting,' cried Daisy.

The twins bawled all the louder.

'I expect they are hungry,' remarked Granny Mulhern.

'Good old Gran!' the twins both thought.

Bill got up and got two bottles ready for them. The babies gulped down the warm milk greedily.

After some time the visitors left.

Next morning the twins awoke to the sound of another screech.

'What is it this time?' shouted Bill from upstairs.

'It's Caspar,' shouted a delighted Dottie, 'and he has three pups with him.'

'Then *he* is not a *he*,' shouted down Bill.

'Are you sure it is our Caspar and not some other dog?'

'Do I look stupid to you?' was the next remark.

'Definitely!' thought Dessie. At this stage he had despaired. Imagine not knowing if

the dog was a boy or a girl! Then panic set in. If the Mulherns were that mixed up maybe they had mistaken the twins as well. Maybe he was a girl and Daisy was a boy! A moment of blind panic overtook him. Then Daisy reminded him that the nurses in the hospital would know. Dessie lay back on his pillow relieved.

At breakfast the twins were ignored. The centre of attention was the returned Caspar with her three pups. The Mulherns had now accepted they had indeed made a mistake and that Caspar was a she.

'Sorry old girl,' said Bill, as he stroked the dog. 'We thought you were a boy. Gertie and Nellie were all excited about the names they would choose for the pups.

'I hope they do a better job on it than they did with us,' remarked Daisy to Dessie.

'I don't care what you call them,' remarked Dottie, 'as long as you find new owners for them and quickly. We have enough hungry mouths to feed,' and she looked with con-tempt at the twins in the corner.

The Twins are Christened

'What do we do now'? asked Dottie of Bill one evening as they sat in the sitting room. 'Do we invite those posh geezers back to the twins christening or do we not?'

'She is talking about Malcolm's parents I think,' hissed Dessie across to Daisy.

'I hope she doesn't,' hissed back Daisy. 'We would never be able to live down the shame of it!'

However, Dottie and Bill decided that Malcolm's parents would need to be asked. It would make the neighbours jealous and besides, maybe it was time they had a few 'upper crust' friends, reasoned Dottie.

'I hope you two know the bother and expense you are putting me to,' scolded Dottie later, as she changed the twins nappies.

'Ignore her!' whispered Dessie. 'She is just trying to send us on a guilt trip again.'

Dessie wished that a nurse would be sent around all parents of new babies to remind them of a baby's need of modesty. There he was, listening to her, with his legs splayed in the air and the whole world could look on again at what should be the most private part of his body. He felt it worse when girls were around and Daisy agreed with his view on it. She felt most uncomfortable when she was in the same situation.

The little attention that they had been getting had almost disappeared. The pups were now the centre of attention. Imagine putting pups before one's babies. Daisy and Dessie were disgusted.

Aunt Norma and Uncle Mervyn would be godparents for Daisy (whatever that was) and Uncle Joe and Aunt Lottie would be godparents for Dessie. The two Grannies and Granda Brown would help with the cooking. Gertie and Nellie would babysit any children who came. Gertie scowled over at the twins.

'I hope you two are happy now. All this effort is your fault.' Daisy could feel tears in her eyes.

'I don't want to babysit a crowd of little squawling brats,' scolded Nellie. 'Why can't Dad do it?'

'Your Dad will be helping me to entertain the guests,' replied Dottie.

'What does entertain mean?' Daisy asked Dessie.

'I don't know,' answered Dessie, 'but I hope the guests are easily pleased.'

Food and drink had to be ordered next. Dottie sent Bill off to a place called the 'Credit Union' to see if he could get a loan.

'What is that?' asked Daisy.

'I think they are short of money,' hissed back Dessie.

'We will need lots of goodies and sweets,' shouted Nellie.

'She is only thinking of herself,' thought Daisy.

Dottie decided that the sitting room would need to be painted. Uncle Mervyn offered to paint and Lottie said she would loan Dottie some new curtains. The twins were ignored for the next few days. Uncle Mervyn had found some cheap paint at the market. There was only one problem. It was a sick mustard colour but Dottie said that it would help brighten the place up. Aunt Lottie sent a pair of red curtains around

'Oh dear! That doesn't match,' said Dottie, but then she had what she called a bright idea. 'I will get a few red cushions and a red plant or two. That will look nice.'

Bill was sent to cut the grass and sort the garden. The girls had to scrub the shower and toilet and clean the bathroom.

Then they stuck up decorations called balloons and streamers.

After a few days the house was cleaner, even if the colours were a bit loud, but the smell of new paint was everywhere.

'Open all the windows,' ordered Dottie, 'or else they will know that we painted the house especially for the christening.'

'That would be bright of them,' thought Dessie, 'especially as the smell of new paint is everywhere.'

The day of the christening arrived. Malcolm's parents arrived carrying Malcolm in his carry cot.

'They look very toffee nosed,' Daisy could hear one of the neighbours say about

Malcolm's folks and she felt sure that Malcolm's parents heard the remark too.

During the afternoon the twins were to meet many new faces, among them Fibber Lonergan, Spice Casey, and Mags Malone, school friends of Gertie and Nellie. However, the one who interested Dessie most was the one called Desmond. Dessie remembered how Gertie had said in the hospital that he was called Dessie after that pimply little fellow called Desmond.

'This must be that geezer!' he thought. He looked over at a little wimp of a fellow that looked as if he wanted to apologise for his very existence. He definitely did-n't look like the type of person that Gertie or Nellie would be friends with?

As the adults were eating at the table Malcolm let off a very loud wail. Gertie and Nellie were supposed to be babysit-ting. Dessie could hear Nellie shout 'Little cry baby' at him as his parents came run-ning. Apparently Spice Casey had drawn a moustache on Malcolm with a black marker and Malcolm was having none of it. Malcolm's parents seemed to be disgusted and Malcolm turned to Daisy and Dessie.

'That should do the trick to get us out of here.' His plan worked.

It was! Malcolm's parents made their excuses and left. Instead of scolding Gertie and Nellie for allowing it all to happen, Dottie said 'Good riddance! We are not good enough for them. Well! They can go and take their snotty little brat with them!'

Bill tried to hush her up as he whispered 'There are people listening'.

'Good!' shouted Dottie, even louder this time. Gertie and Nellie began to giggle as did Spice Casey, Mags Malone, Fibber Lonergan and pimply Desmond.

The twins slid down further under their blanket. They were so embarrassed they wanted to hide.

Daily Life at the Mulherns

Dessie looked with longing at Gertie's mobile phone the next morning as she texted her friend. He knew you could send messages on these things and he longed to text Malcolm to say 'sorry' for the hurt caused to him and his family.

Dottie was not in a good mood as she looked around at the litter, the empty bottles and cans, and the leftover food.

'Thinking of the whole thing gives me a headache,' she said, as she took a tablet with a drink of water. 'Be a dear Bill and clean it up for me. I am going back to bed.'

The twins had already noticed that whenever there was a lot of work that needed to be done Dottie was always ill. By mid morning, Bill had the place cleaned up.

'How nice and peaceful the house is,' thought Daisy, 'without Gertie, Nellie and Dottie.' Gertie and Nellie had gone downtown to put up posters in the shop windows saying 'Pups for sale'. The twins had heard them discussing it with Bill before they left.

'How much should we charge?' asked Nellie. Bill laughed.

'Did you say charge? You will be lucky if you get giving those three mutts away. I mean, look at their mother.'

'There is nothing wrong with Caspar,' sulked Gertie, 'except that you and Mum gave her that stupid name on her thinking she was a boy.'

Bill was embarrassed. 'I have written down "Three pedigree pups for sale – price on request",' continued Gertie.

The twins had to agree with Bill. They

had seen the three pups and weren't too impressed.

Gertie and Nellie slammed the door behind them as they went out. Dessie was certain that all those banging noises were bound to have an effect on him and Daisy in later years.

Dottie was in a much better mood when she woke up and discovered that Bill had all the work done.

'As a special treat,' she said, 'I will make us something nice for tea and you can put your feet up.'

'Oh no!' thought the twins. Every time Dottie began to cook the smell of burning food went through the house. Gertie and Nellie often seemed to pretend they weren't hungry and even Caspar whimpered under the table when she took out his doggie dish.

'Well, at least she can't burn our milk, or can she?' asked Dessie. Daisy giggled.

'This was as near a perfect day as one could get in the Mulhern house,' she thought. However, there still was a crisis to come!

After tea everyone went into the sitting room for what Dottie called a family meeting. The twins could hear Gertie hiss on the way in, 'I don't like the sound of this'. When they were all seated Dottie explained that the time had come for their Dad Bill to go back to work. Granny had everything arranged though.

'I will stay here during the week and Gertie and Nellie can help with the babies at the weekends. It's all arranged.'

Gertie and Nellie scowled over at the twins but said nothing. As Granny left the room, Gertie and Nellie stuck their tongues out at her. They were too scared to argue with her though.

When things had settled Dottie switched on the television. Suddenly it blinked and went off. The light too went out.

The twins could hear Bill say, 'Oh no! we have a power cut'.

Then Dottie asked crossly, 'Bill, did you pay the ESB bill recently?' Bill looked sheepish.

'I don't believe this!' complained Nellie.

'Just when my film was about to start.'

'Trust her to think only of herself,' whispered Dessie. Bill went looking for what he called 'candles' and he lit them. Daisy and Dessie found the candlelight strangely peaceful. Just then, there was a knock on the sitting-room window. The Reverend was peering in at them.

'What is he nosing at now?' scowled Gertie.

'He sure picks his moments,' complained Bill, as he went into the hall to let him in.

'I just called for a friendly visit,' the Reverend said. 'My word, it is dark in here.' No one moved to give the Reverend a seat or to welcome him.

'We just thought that it would be cosy to sit in the candlelight your Reverence,' replied Dottie quickly. 'You know, to get back to nature, that sort of thing!'

'Quite! Quite!' murmured the Reverend looking at her strangely. 'Well! Perhaps I will call some other day when it is more convenient. He quickly headed towards the door.

'Now Gertie!' scolded Dottie, when he had left the room. 'Pull those curtains before someone else sees us sitting in the dark. We will be disgraced if the neighbours find out!'

'Keep your hair on,' answered Gertie angrily. 'It's not our fault you don't pay your bills on time.' Then with 'C'mon Nellie', she and Nellie stormed out of the room.

'That's what I call a more normal day with the Mulherns,' laughed Dessie, as he and Daisy had a good giggle under the blanket.

The Twins Get an Injection

A few days later Dottie announced to the twins that she was taking them for their injection.

'What is an injection?' wondered Dessie. He knew that Daisy wouldn't know either. All he could do was keep his ear to the ground and try and pick up some clues from listening to Bill and Dottie.

The first clue was that it was something horrid was when he heard Bill say, 'Just as well they don't know where you are taking them!' Then much later he heard Bill and Lottie discussing injections.

'Rather them than ne,' said Bill. Dessie pricked up his ears.

'Nonsense!' replied Dottie. 'They are two fine healthy babies. It won't do them one bit of harm.'

Dessie thought it better not to tell Daisy. He didn't want to worry her.

After lunch the twins were bathed and dressed in two matching baby suits. Then Dottie put them in the pram and wheeled them down the town until she came to a place called 'The Surgery'. At least that is what the sign said. Dessie could feel his little heart beating with fright.

'What was this injection that he and Daisy were going to get?' He just didn't trust Dottie. He was to find out soon enough.

Inside there were lots of other babies with their mothers. Daisy could see Lauren with her mum and waved to her. Each time a little bell rang and a light flashed, another mother got up from her seat and left the room. Soon it was Dottie's turn. They walked down a long corridor and came to a door with 'Doctor' written on it.

'Come in', they heard just as they reached the door. Inside sat a lady in a white coat who smiled at the twins.

The horror of what happened next is something that neither Daisy nor Dessie will ever forget. The lady took out a long needle and held it up in front of the twins.

'I wonder why she is showing us that?' thought the twins. They soon found out. She pulled down each baby's nappy in turn and stuck the sharp needle into their bottoms. Daisy and Dessie shrieked with pure fright.

'Sensitive little things, aren't they?' remarked the doctor. Dessie was too sore to get annoyed at the word 'things'. He got more annoyed when Dottie answered 'Oh! just like their father, the pair of them! Can't take any pain.'

'That is rich!' thought Daisy. We should be delighted that someone is sticking a long sharp needle into us?' She was fuming with rage.

'Get your own back Daisy,' commanded Dessie. 'Bawl as loud as you can.'

Daisy and Dessie screeched until their lungs almost burst.

'See what I told you,' said Dottie to the doctor. 'Just like their father,' and she left the surgery.

The twins had so exhausted themselves screeching that they slept the whole way home. In her dream Daisy could see Dottie and Lottie lining up for a jab. This time, however, it wasn't the doctor who was giv- ing the jab but Dessie. He had a huge smile on his face.

When they got home Bill told Dottie to leave the twins in the sitting room as he had the tea ready. Dottie wheeled the pram into the sitting room and then went into the kitchen. A lovely smell of frying bacon came out to where the twins were. Their mouths began to water.

'That was another thing about Dottie

116

and Bill,' thought Dessie. 'They had no consideration for others. Surely he and Daisy should get fed first even if it was only a bottle.'

When Gertie and Nellie came in they were told how the twins had disgraced their mother at the doctors.

'What did you expect them to do?' asked Nellie cheekily. 'Laugh and ask for more?'

Dottie Goes to the Gym

Next day Dottie slept late as usual. When she arrived downstairs Dottie and Daisy had been fed and changed. They knew that she was in one of her moods.

'Look what those two did to me!' she said and pointed her finger in their direction.

'What two?' wondered Dessie, as he peered out.

'I have put on at least a stone,' continued Dottie 'and my legs are all veins. I am joining the gym.'

That afternoon she arrived into the

sitting-room in a very tight track suit. Her fat legs were wedged into squeaky new runners and she had a silly looking hair band around her head.

'Right! You two! You are coming with me,' she said to the twins. 'We are going to the gym.'

They went down town until they came to a large building. Inside were lots of people of all shapes and sizes. Some were jumping into a large pool of water, some were walking or running on strange looking machines, others were just watching.

After leaving the twins in a room which said 'Crèche' on the door Dottie went out to the large exercise area. There was a glass wall and the twins could see her through it.

'It would be hard not to see her,' whispered Daisy to Dessie.

Dottie stepped on to the walking machine. At first everything looked normal but then the twins noticed something odd. The machine was going faster and

Dottie was getting warmer. They saw her pressing on a button at the side.

'I think she is trying to stop,' said Dessie.

Daisy thought Dottie was beginning to look strange. Her face was getting redder and redder, and sweat was pouring from her face. Next they heard the shriek.

'Help! I can't stop this thing,' she wailed. The twins thought they would die laughing. A man went over and stopped the machine. Dottie did not look well. She was scolding the man but the twins couldn't hear it all through the glass wall.

The next time they saw Dottie was when they saw her standing on a board beside the large pool of water.

'I think she is going to jump in,' said

Daisy feeling a little nervous. They didn't have too long to wait. A large splash hit the pool and the water splashed out on all sides.

By the time the twins arrived home Dottie was hardly able to walk. She staggered into the house and stood on a little metal box in the corner.

'I am still the same weight,' she wailed, 'and it's all because of those two. I put on all that weight when I was pregnant.'

'I think she means us,' whispered Dessie. 'We are blamed for everything round here,' whispered Dessie.

'Now!,now,' Bill consoled his wife. 'You will soon see the weight come off if you eat more salads and cut out the fatty food like chocolate and ice-cream.'

'What do you mean?' asked Dottie, crossly. 'Are you saying I'm fat?'

'Of course I'm not,' stammered Bill nervously.

'Liar,' thought Daisy. That was another thing about adults that she and Dessie had noticed. They never seemed to be happy. Even if Dottie was a little overweight, so what?

When Gertie and Nellie asked Bill later where Dottie was he told them that she had gone off to bed with a box of chocolates in a huff!

Dottie was up early the next morning. She was dressed in the same outfit as before. However, instead of wolfing down a few rounds of tea and toast Dottie just drank a glass of orange juice. Then she said she was going jogging. The twins could just see the top of her head bobbing up and down as she went past the window.

'That is it,' said Gertie to Nellie out loud as they came into the kitchen for breakfast. 'Our mum has finally lost her marbles.'

'She didn't say anything about losing marbles to us, did she Dessie?' Daisy asked Dessie who finally understood that adults never said what they meant.

'I think they have all lost their marbles,' Dessie replied.

After a few days of nibbling lettuce leaves and raw carrots, after hours of jogging and many visits to the gym, Dottie finally gave up.

'I don't think I am meant to be thin,' she announced one morning at breakfast. 'Anyway, who wants to be a sickly looking little knitting needle of a thing?'

'You could have fooled us,' thought Dessie. 'We were sure you did!'

That ended the crying outbursts and the strange moods she had been in for the past few days. Dottie went back to stuffing herself with chocolate and to lying in front of the television.

The twins heard Bill tell Granny Mulhern on the phone that Dottie and her diet was driving him around the bend. The twins had never seen Dottie driving but felt sure that Bill wouldn't say such a thing if it wasn't true.

Life continued in this way for the twins until one morning Gertie and Nellie announced that the twins were almost six months old and that maybe they should have another party? The twins lay back in their pram and hoped that Dottie would

say a very firm no!

As it happened that is exactly what she did but not before reminding Gertie and Nellie of how much the twins had cost her so far. Pleased, Daisy and Dessie lay back in their pram and began to think back over the last six months.

A lot had happened to them in that time. They had come into the world. They had got to know their strange family. They had made friends with Malcolm, Megan and Lauren. They had been introduced to their unusual relatives. They had been to a christening party. They had been kidnapped. They had been given two new name, Daisy and Dessie. They had survived in a family where, at times, the dog was thought more of than they. They had also won a Bonny Baby prize.

The twins had come to realise that love is more important than money. Malcolm taught them that. They now knew that happiness came from loving and being loved. Their friends Megan and Lauren were sure signs of that. Also, they understood that most adults hardly ever mean what they say or say what they mean.

Another discovery they had made was that they were not like ordinary kids. Even Gran had noticed that. They seemed to have a higher intelligence than many of the babies or indeed adults around them.

What did the future hold, they wondered. Only time would tell!